Bedtime for Bear

Bedtime for Bear

STORY BY **Sandol Stoddard**

ILLUSTRATED BY **Lynn Munsinger**

1985

HOUGHTON MIFFLIN COMPANY

Library of Congress Cataloging in Publication Data

Stoddard, Sandol.
  Bedtime for bear.

  Summary: Small bear uses every excuse to avoid going
to bed much to the exasperation of Big bear.
  1. Children's stories, American. [1. Bedtime—
Fiction. 2. Bears—Fiction] I. Munsinger, Lynn, ill.
II. Title.
PZ7.S868Be 1985   [E]   85-5259
ISBN 0-395-38811-2

Printed in the United States of America
H 10 9 8 7 6 5 4 3 2 1

I can't go to sleep,
said Small.

Why not?
asked Big.

Because the upstairs dark
is different from the dark downstairs,
and it's not the right kind of dark there at all
for bears, said Small.
And I am a bear.

Oh my, said Big.
Whatever shall we do?
Shall I make a little lair

for a very small bear
downstairs tonight
right next to mine?

That would be fine, said Small.
And it was.

But pretty soon…
I can't go to sleep,
Small said,
because I hear a noise,
a very big noise,
and the noise I am hearing is bees,
and bears don't like bees one bit.
And I am a bear.

The bees are tucked in, said Big.
They have turned out the light.
The bees are all sound asleep
at this time of night.
Why aren't you?

Because it isn't fair, Small said.

Even in my lair

I've tried to sing and I've tried to hum,

but I need something else and

I need a thumb.

But I haven't got a thumb because because

bears only have paws.

And I'm a bear.

Hush, said Big.
Paws are delicious
with a little yogurt and brown sugar on them —
there!

And that was true,

but pretty soon…

I really am a bear,
said Small, I am —
and bears don't like going to bed at all,
and they don't fit in beds that are big

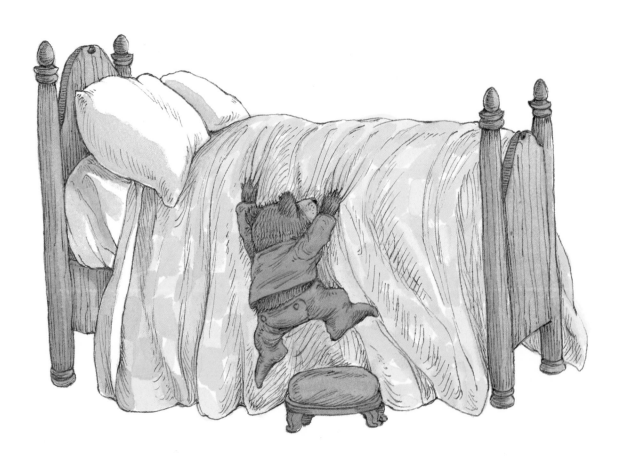

or beds that are small,

and they need a drink of water all the time,

and especially they don't like wearing
scratchy pajamas.

Heavens! cried Big,
I never heard of such a thing.
All the bears I know go to bed at 6 P.M.
and they are never thirsty

and they all wear red pajamas with feet in them
just like yours.

Go to sleep now, little bear,
Go — go to sleep!

But I don't want to go,
whispered Small pretty soon.
I want to stay.

Because what a bear really needs
is another bear.

One that will never go away,
especially in the night.

I am here, whispered Big.

I am here, my own dear little bear.

And I will never, never go away.

Yes, said Small,

I know.

But I need somebody to hold me.

Oh terrible bear, cried Big, oh bear of mine,

you are not small at all, you are huge,

you are the loudest noise I ever hear,

you are the most enormous pest.

Why do I still love you best

when of all the bears in town tonight

you are the very, very worst?

Then in the big-small rocking chair
in the right kind of dark
for any size bear,
they rocked and they rocked and they rocked...

And guess which one of them
fell asleep first?